I0517413

Odds & Socks

A Selection of Short Stories

by
T. L. Cowell

McKnight & Bishop Ltd

Image Credits

All images used are either in the public domain or have been used with permission where no attribution or credit is needed with the following exceptions:

ISBN 978-1-905691-30-2

A CIP catalogue record for this book is available from the British Library

First published in 2014 by McKnight & Bishop Ltd.

McKnight & Bishop Ltd.
28 Grifffiths Court, Bowburn, Co. Durham, DH6 5FD
http://www.mcknightbishop.com
info@mcknightbishop.com

This books has been typeset in Garamond and ParmaPetit

Printed and bound in Great Britain by Bonacia Ltd, Peterborough

for
Joyce Cowell

and
Sheila Dryden

About the Author

You can find T. L. Cowell on Twitter as *@tlcwrites*, on Facebook (*T. L. Cowell*) and on tumblr as *tlcowellwrites*.

T. L. Cowell lives in Norfolk, UK, with her personal petting zoo and family. She fights chronic headache, migraine, anxiety and depression, and several other conditions on a daily basis. She lives with her head in the clouds, feet on the ground and nose in a book. *Odds & Socks, A Selection of Short Stories* is her first publication.

She recommends T. Morgan Editing Services to anyone looking for an exceptional editor. T. Morgan can be found at their website, http://www.tmorganediting.weebly.com and is currently open for commissions.

Please keep an eye out for her next publications – *Pick & Mix, A Selection of Short Stories* and the debut novel, *Alpha*, both coming soon.

About The Publisher

McKnight & Bishop are always on the lookout for great new authors and ideas for exciting new books. If you write or if you have an idea for a book, email us:
info@mcknighbishop.com

Some things we love are: undiscovered authors, open-source software, crowd-funding, Amazon/Kindle, social networking, faith, laughter and new ideas.

Visit us at: **www.mcknightbishop.com**

Contents

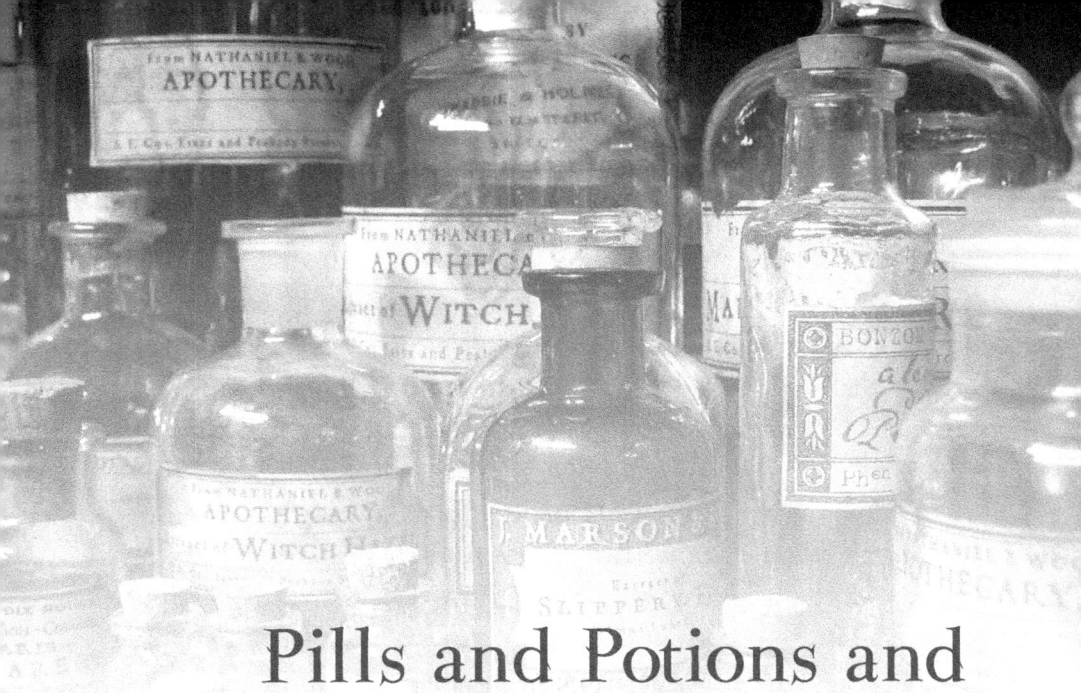

Pills and Potions and Whatchamacallits

There are snapshots of stories hidden everywhere. Hee hee hee, you don't believe me, do you? You think I'm making it up, that I'm a crazy old lady with an overactive imagination. Do you think I didn't get enough attention when I was little, or maybe that I was dropped on the head as a babe? Maybe, you even think I have a Seeing Eye; that I'm psychic and get visions of the future.

After all, you and your little friends keep coming back for more tales, don't you? You can't get enough of them, with your greedy little grabbing paws, sniffling noses, and hopeful eyes.

Or maybe, just maybe, you think this is all witchcraft. Hocus pocus, jiggery pokery and alakazam. The kind of tricks that a wizard can pull out of their sleeve. You're not expecting me to pull a rabbit out of my hat, now, are you?

Oh, don't sit there. That's Mister's chair. He doesn't like it if a scamp like you sits in his chair. He'll set his green eyes on you and his black fur will puff up like magic. Maybe he'll even unsheathe those claws of his and with the twitch of his whiskers, unleash his fury on you. He's an old moggie; he believes anything is his to own.

Oho, anyway, if you do believe that I'm magic (and I can tell; I can see it in those twitchy eyes), then I'm afraid I'm not up to all that much. My cantrips are lacklustre, my chants abysmal, and my potions merely amount to a darn good cup of tea. Mind you, you should never doubt the importance of a good cup of tea. It can work wonders, you know.

But, I must ask you. Why have you come to seek me out, specifically? Every human being is a storyteller. Or at least, they should be. Some people just bury that instinct under pointless trivia like facts and logic and duty. Are my tales really that much better? Are my snacks really tastier than the sweet and savoury treats that anyone else can offer you?

You children are young; you should be enjoying the outdoors. Go, stretch your legs, watch the clouds pass by and scare some pigeons. Play with your pet pooch or younger siblings. You don't really want to be cooped up with an old ninny like me, do you?

Or perhaps, you do? Perhaps you are looking for shocking stories to take home to your sceptical parents. Perhaps they are looking for an excuse to kick me out of my old family home? Perhaps you are just here digging for dirt.

Let me tell you, it won't work. Do you know why? It's simple, really. Your parents have been here before you. They came for my sweets and tricks and tales of yore. They know every trick in the book. On the contrary, they expect their babes to come crawling into my arms sooner or later. It's the fate of everyone who lives in this village, you see.

They say that my snacks have a magical quality to them. Apparently, my cough drops really do cure that hacking cough. And my cookies? They can help even the most troublesome case of insomnia. Don't worry about it; it may be true or it may not. Really, it's all just everyday magic. Haha, it's the kind of thing that anyone can do with a little application and a little faith. Even my cat; there're rumours that he is a witch's cat. Does that make me a witch or am I really just a humble old lady telling my stories for free? Is Mister simply an old gentleman, looking for somewhere to rest during his winter years?

Ahh, I need to get back to the point. The power of hope and thought knows no bounds. If you think something is true, then it is far more likely to be so. Oho, you should never underestimate the power of the human mind. Especially not you lot, not at your age. This is when your imagination runs riot and that means you have a greater capacity to touch the magic hidden in the world. Ageing is a terrible thing; you'll grow more and more mundane if you don't cultivate your imagination now.

So come, let your mind bloom and grow. Hee hee, I am certainly willing to help you all. It's your choice if you believe or not.

Here, let me show you a photograph. Yes, yes. It's old; please do be careful. It's my only copy. I don't want to see any tea stains or tears on it, thank you very much.

What do you see? Please, tell me what you think of it. I want to know if you can tell what the stories are within this photograph. Believe me, there are many. You just need to know how to look at it.

It's old and blurry? You can't see anything because of that? Is that really all you have to say? Well of *course* it is blurry. Technology has come such a long way. Haha, yes, in some ways that's a good thing, but it does destroy some of the magic in the world. Those computers in your pockets and the technological whatsadoodles you have at home? They are nothing like the equipment used to take this picture.

Oho, I'll tell you some of the stories, then. Just a snapshot of them, mind. I don't want you to know all of the secrets too quickly. Otherwise, why would you even bother to come back? That's another kind of magic; knowing when to start and when to stop. It's powerful, if you know how to use it. It's the power that keeps me going. The more people need me, the more my will for survival kicks in.

You over there, yeah, the laddie with the black curly hair and chocolate skin. Take a lemon sweet. It'll help your sore throat. And you, the one at the back who can't sit still? Please, have a cupcake. Yes, the taste is slightly unusual; the chamomile will do that. But it'll grow on you and you never know what else it'll do.

Are you all settled? Mister, you settle down as well. I'll get you a saucer of milk after these kiddies have received what they came here for. Good, now everybody is ready, I'll begin.

This photograph, yes. It's still the starting point in the tale. No, no, I'm not interested in anything that's pictured. Let us look at something else. Hee, how about the camera itself? The camera could well have many, many stories to tell.

Who owned it? When was it made? What exactly has it seen? What other photographs has it taken for posterity? Has the camera been destroyed or is it in a museum now? Maybe, just maybe, it has been handed down to yet another temporary guardian. It could even still be in use. After all, in those times, things were built to last.

So, let's not even think about the camera itself now. Ha, yes, let's think about the person who made it. Imagine, a man with greying hair and sad eyes. His wife is dying. He's giving her all he can to keep her healthy. He gives her peppermint to soothe her stomach, lemon and honey to calm her painful throat. Then there is lavender to help her sleep, feverfew, liquorice, marshmallow and nettle to ease her aching joints.

But this backyard magic won't keep her alive. He wants, no, he *needs* to remember. He simply has to honour every wrinkle on her face, the sparkle in her eyes and the glow of her hair.

What ways can he memorialise his love? He could write down every mole and every eyelash. But that, of course, relies on human imagination. Every mind sees something differently. Oho, yes, that's the magic of humanity. People's brains are all different and that's a good thing. However, it doesn't help when telling the story of a person and their beauty. It just has too many variables.

Poetry? Haha, of course that has the same issue as prose. Hee, it may evoke a person's sentiment with ease. However, does it really portray a person as a whole properly? It leaves too many blanks. Even if it were a song or a saga, it cuts too many corners. Ha, this will never do for our poor man.

After all, he is already mourning for his love's death before she has passed on. It's terribly sad. All he wants to do is cling onto her for that little bit longer. He needs something to remember her by after she's gone. Yes, he has his memories but they fade as time marches on. That's just a part of the natural order of things. Magic, if you will.

What about painting his wife? Believe me, he's tried. Oho, how he has tried. But each picture he paints has a fault or a flaw which distracts from the whole. He's never satisfied. He always has to start again, to make it right. But it'll never be right. Even the greatest of painters can struggle to convey true realism. It's near-on impossible for a rank amateur to paint like, ha, well, like a photograph.

But. But, but, but. He's heard of new technology. He has to try it himself. Our gentleman, who is preparing for the death of his wife, ha, he's a clever, wily old gent. He's an architect, a designer, an inventor, or maybe, just a tinkerer. Oho, it doesn't matter really what he ranks himself as. What matters is that he manages to make this camera.

It means he can finally have a memento of his wife he is satisfied with. Yes, the camera may well be antiquated, ha, and yes, a little blurry. Hee hee, but it still portrays her and it's the best he can do at this moment in time.

Ah, but the photograph doesn't show an elderly woman? Haha, no, you're quite right; it doesn't. What it does show is something entirely different. But this isn't the story hidden within this specific photograph. This is a story of the camera which took this photograph. Heh, specifically, this is the story of its creation.

Is it true? Haha, does it matter if it's true or not? The point remains: there are stories everywhere. You just have to use your noggin to unearth them.

Oh my, oho, look at the time. Your parents will start wondering whatever has happened to you. Maybe they are inventing all sorts of stories due to your disappearance. They might have an inkling of what the truth is, ha, but their minds will take tangents. See? Stories and magic are everywhere.

You want more stories? You want to know more about the camera and the photograph? You need to know what else I can see? Haha, I told you. This is my magic. You want more; you need to come back.

But for now: out, out, out. Not another word, I grant you. I'm an old lady and I'm nearing my bed time. I need to rest my aching bones. I need to feed Mister; he gets angry if he doesn't have his dinner on time. Heh, I cannot deal with a sulking moggie.

So, off with you, you little rabble. Come back some other day. I'll see what I can cook up for you then. I mean, I'm not going anywhere any time soon.

Stargazer

The stars danced across the sky. Twinkling pinpoints of light, billions of miles away.

Nathanael knew that the stars weren't really twinkling at all; it was just an illusion created by the atmosphere around the planet. Instead, the light was a function of chemical reactions, and it took more than a lifetime to get to the planet. The facts behind the phenomena made the sight all the more awe-inspiring to Nathaniel. Every time he looked at the night sky, the vision took his breath away.

He jolted to a sudden stop as the brakes were applied to his wheelchair. Nathaniel sighed. He hated being so restricted. He loathed the fact that people thought there was something wrong with his mind just because he was stuck in a chair. It wasn't the case and he knew it. If people asked him virtually anything about astronomy, he knew the answer. On the rare occasions that he didn't, he would make the effort to research it.

Fingertips ran over his black curls. The feel of his mother's hand through his hair gave Nathaniel mixed feelings. On the one hand, he enjoyed the comfort of knowing that he had a close bond with his mum. On the other, he found it terribly patronising and wished that she could see that he was a teenager now. Just because he needed help getting around sometimes, it didn't mean that he was a baby anymore.

"Is this all right, baby?" she whispered soothingly. Nathaniel nodded once. He could barely see his mother's face. Only the glow of the full moon illuminated it. She looked ghostly, ethereal. Only a wisp of a woman was left now. It broke Nathaniel's heart.

This was one of her rare nights off. As a night-shift worker in a care home, his mum didn't really ever see the light of day. Even on her days off, she spent the nights awake and felt like she still had to work. At the care home, she was Aminifu Davies, the night nurse and general dogsbody. As soon as she was back at home, Aminifu became his mother and full-time carer. She had no time for herself, never mind getting the chance to bask in the warm glow of a sunny day. Sometimes, Nathaniel believed the night was her natural territory, but there were times when he could see the fear in her eyes.

He often felt guilty, too. After all, whenever it was dry and the night was clear, he insisted that she bring him outside. Their tiny back garden wasn't good enough, no. There was too much light pollution in the city. How could he observe the majesty of the night sky if it was being polluted by the ghastly glow of the street lamps? Instead, Nathaniel asked her to drive him to the middle of the darkest fields and set up his telescope so he could observe.

She had sacrificed so much for him. Nathaniel knew it and felt the guilt intensely. He didn't have to ask her questions, or pry into her personal life. He just knew. His mum was always there for him, rain or shine. She worked gruelling hours just to keep a roof over their heads. She paid for him to have the best medical care. Even his wheelchair was state of the art.

But, she needed a life outside of him and work. Although she never complained, Nathaniel knew that his mother was lonely. His father was 'out of the equation' as she tactfully put it. He had never felt the need for another parental figure because his mum fulfilled the role of both without batting an eyelid.

"Nate, baby, are you okay?" she crooned and rubbed his shoulders affectionately. "You're very quiet tonight."

"I'm fine, Mum. Are you?"

"Of course I'm all right." She never told the truth. The sadness and the loneliness in her eyes betrayed her. "Now, shall we get your telescope set up for a spot of stargazing?"

Nathaniel nodded. He watched with eagle eyes as his mum struggled to put up the folding table. He wished he could help her, but with legs unable to operate, he knew that he was more of a hindrance than a help. All he could do was keep the torch trained on the table so his mum had a thin slither of unnatural light to assist her.

When the case to the telescope was drawn out from the rucksack that hung on the back of his wheelchair, Nathaniel's eyes lit up. For a moment, he forgot all of his guilt, filled with sheer exuberance and joy for astronomy.

He had tried to go to an observatory and join an astronomy club. Wheelchair access, however, was utterly dismal and prevented him from getting any further. Nathaniel still grimaced at the memory. The sheer injustice never settled well.

Why should he—and many other people just like him—be prevented from following their dreams simply because of their physical, mental, or emotional limitations?

All he wanted to do was astronomy. Nathaniel swore he was going to make some great discoveries in the field. He wanted to be the astronomer who discovered amazing things, maybe even life on other planets. Yes, he knew that he had to work incredibly hard at his physics and mathematics in order to get that far, but he was trying. No, he was determined to get there in the end. He didn't care how many years he had to try. He had to make his family proud of him.

For now, though, he was completely indebted to his mother for helping him dabble in it as a hobby.

"Orion's belt looks bright tonight, Nate," his mum observed as he lovingly stroked the telescope and made the appropriate adjustments.

He nodded absentmindedly. His attention fell entirely onto the telescope. Nothing else could draw his focus away. There was meant to be a meteor shower starting up soon. Nathaniel shivered with excitement. He didn't even notice as his mother set up her own fold-out chair and settled down quietly beside him.

She wasn't very good with the whole astronomy thing. She could identify a few constellations and pick out the North Star, but that was about it. Even telling apart a planet from a star was beyond her. Still, as much as Nathaniel found her obliviousness irksome, he still adored her. Without her, he wouldn't have been here at all.

Once, she had told him the story about his father. He had wanted to put Nathaniel up for adoption days after he was born. As soon as he realised that his son was disabled, he wanted nothing to do with him. He believed that Nathaniel was broken, faulty, and therefore, completely worthless.

His mother had fought for him. It had ended their marriage, but she always asserted that it was completely worth it. She told him time and time again that he was the most precious thing she could ever have.

But Nathaniel still couldn't get rid of the nagging feeling that his birth had ruined her life. If he hadn't been around, then she wouldn't have had to work night after night. It was his fault she was the sole provider for the family. She had to keep food on the table, supply him with clothes and comfort. She allowed him to chase his hobbies and his dreams. That was without the added complications that his disabilities provided. Then there were the constant stream of hospital appointments, physiotherapists, alterations to their home and beyond to take into account.

There was little he hated more than being a burden to his mother. Her husband, his father, hadn't thought he was worth it. She had seen that little spark of potential and was determined to give him everything he needed to achieve it. Singlehandedly, she had taken on far more than the vast majority of people would bother. She had done it without complaint, simply because she loved him.

He had to pay her back. He had to get his astrophysics degree and follow it up with his subsequent path into research.

For now, he had to give her something else. Three months ago, he had logged onto the internet, searched for an appropriate website and filled in a form. Nathaniel had waited impatiently until he got confirmation. Finally, he was ready to show his precious mother just how much he loved her too.

Training his eye through the eyepiece, Nathaniel slowly scanned the night sky. Breath caught in his throat. As beautiful as it was looking at the night sky without additional assistance, there was something about the telescope which made it come alive. This was what he loved about it. It was the freedom to explore without being hindered by literal motion. It didn't matter that his legs didn't work; he could investigate the universe from the comfort of his wheelchair.

Finally, he located the patch of sky that he was looking for. Nathaniel was grateful that they had managed to catch such a clear night. It made everything so much easier. Slowly and surely, he focused his telescope onto a specific star.

"Mum?" he said softly. "Look, look here."

"Why, Nate, baby? You know I'm no good with all this astronomy stuff. I can tell the Plough apart from Orion and that's about it."

Nathaniel clicked his tongue. "You don't have to do anything but look. Please, Mum."

She rolled her eyes and acquiesced. Jiggling around excitably in his chair, Nathaniel instructed himself to calm down under his breath. "You see that star, Mum? Right in the middle?" He waited for her to answer. When she confirmed, he let out a sigh of relief. "Mum, that's your star. It's called HD984654 Aminifudavies."

His mother fell silent for a second, processing the information. Nathaniel couldn't help but wonder what he'd done wrong, she was so quiet. He took a cautious look at her face and she looked almost sad. Guilt sank to the bottom of his stomach like a heavy stone. Yet again, he'd done something wrong.

"Oh, baby," she eventually breathed. "You named a star after me?"

Nervously, he nodded. "B-but, why are you crying?"

She let out a weak smile. "It's perfect. You're perfect. I love you. What did I do to deserve a son as wonderful as you?"

How could he answer a question like that? He certainly didn't feel perfect. The fact that he was in and out of hospital, that his dad never wanted him, that society made him feel pathetic, all of that made him feel incompetent. At least, though, he'd done one thing right.

His mother wrapped her arms tightly around his shoulders. He fell into her hug; really, he had very little choice. If it weren't for her, Nathaniel would believe that all those people who told him he was useless were right. It was because of her that he believed he could actually do something.

"Oh look, a shooting star!" she exclaimed. Nathaniel didn't bother to correct her. "Make a wish, baby. You have to make a wish."

In spite of himself, Nathaniel closed his eyes. He knew exactly what he needed to wish for.

The Secret Lives of Rabbits

Have you heard of the Moon Rabbit?

I expect not, unless you can communicate in the secret language of their species. Tales are important to rabbits. Like humanity, they thrive on stories, myths, and legends. Unlike humans, sometimes, just sometimes, their collective belief can make said stories come true.

The Rabbit in the Moon? Yes, you may have mistaken it for the Man in the Moon, the Sandman; you may have believed that the Moon Rabbit is merely the benevolent face who looks down on the world as we slumber.

It's a common misconception, one that people perpetuate in generation after generation. We humans are selfish beasts; we try to steal what is not ours. We make grandiose claims and expect every other living thing to bend to our whims.

But the Moon Rabbit will never be ours. It doesn't matter how much we want it, or how much we spread our lies about the supposed Man in the Moon, this is one thing we will never have. The belief of the rabbit community is too strong for us to be capable of stealing it from underneath their paws.

I know what you're thinking: rabbits are gentle, quiet creatures. They do not have a violent bone in their body. They break all too easily, but they choose to live simple lives, with simple needs. Everyone knows someone who owns a fat, lazy rabbit who sits in his hutch all day, just chewing grass. This is not how a rabbit would choose to live. Ordinarily, they are vivacious creatures. They have far more to give than people give them credit for.

Rabbits keep so many secrets close to their little bunny hearts. The Moon Rabbit is just the biggest of them all.

Come, listen, and watch with me. You hear that rabbit grinding his teeth? He's purring, contented and happy. He has fresh grass at his disposal and the space to run free. Not all rabbits have these luxuries . He pays homage to the Moon Rabbit in gratitude for all the resources that he has. But his time is limited. There are rabbits in the warren that are diseased. Myxomatosis will take them down one by one. Their last days will be shrouded solely by fear and pain. They won't be able to eat, drink, or even move as their fragile bodies succumb to disease. It is painful, it is terrifying, and no animal should have to suffer this fate. However, like humans have their diseases, rabbits do too. Myths aren't the only thing that we share.

Please, follow me over here now. The doe is shivering, growling. She stands before her litter of newly born kittens. She's a protective guard. She will not stand down. Her babies are relying on her to ensure they make it to adulthood. But, there are threats big and small out in the wild world. Foxes, cats, dogs, birds of prey, and of course, us humans. Rabbits have thousands of predators. It is bred into them to be scared. Their faith in the Moon Rabbit is what keeps them alive.

The hunt is on elsewhere. The rabbit squeals and screams. It's quite possibly the most terrifying sound you will ever hear. This rabbit, this doe, she's just a child. She's trying to leave the warren; it's overcrowded and if she even bothers to mate, she'll just reabsorb her kittens. The grass is greener on the other side for a doe like her.

However, leaving the warren is fraught with danger. She's already caught herself up into a spot of bother. Specifically, one of the many traditional enemies of the rabbit: foxes. We should leave quickly. I can guarantee that blood will be spilled. This doe may have some powerful defences at her disposal, but that doesn't mean she'll survive.

After all, this is the way of life for animals that are considered to be mere prey.

Just because she's about to die, doesn't mean that she lacks her faith. This doe knows that the Moon Rabbit will take her home. Her body may be surrendered to the fox, but her soul will travel to a place where she is safe and contented. This is one thing all rabbits agree on: one day, the Moon Rabbit will come and collect them. Safety is on the other side of the moon. For now, they have to face the dangers of the world.

Even pet rabbits aren't excluded from terror. Being picked up instinctively reminds them of the threat of a hawk. The vast majority are neglected and ignored; unlike their wild counterparts, they are starved and forgotten about. They die, surrounded by their own excrement and filth. The diseases of the wild rabbits can still take them down. Literally freezing to death is not uncommon.

That's enough about the terror that rabbits suffer on this planet. It is a depressing and stark reality. But, it doesn't mean that rabbits cannot find joy in life. It doesn't mean their lives are worthless, that they are born to die in one of so many violent ways.

Look, there are pet rabbits that are spoilt rotten. Spayed and neutered, they are free from the maddening hormones which they are famed for. The need to reproduce cannot kill them anymore. Vaccines protect them from disease. Responsible owners give them love and attention, good food and space to run. These rabbits live the good life and purr in gratitude to the Moon Rabbit.

Rabbit ears are alive and alert, almost like they have a mind of their own, picking up every sound. Watch how they twitch, how they move. The amazing sense of hearing they have, that's something which helps to keep them alive. This gift was inherited, of course, from the Moon Rabbit. They spend their lives listening for any signs of the Moon Rabbit. It's also why they are diurnal; up at dawn and dusk. In the evenings, they greet the moon and in the mornings, they bid it farewell.

The nose twitch; it's one of their methods of communication. As a mostly silent species, they sacrificed their noise in favour of quietude. It means they are less noticeable to prey, they can creep and crawl undetected. But they talk, they know how one another feels and it is how they share the story of the Moon Rabbit. Nothing spreads the word faster than a simple nose twitch. The stamping, meanwhile, is merely reserved for frustration or fear; anything that is worthy of alarm. It wouldn't honour the Moon Rabbit to thump its name.

And, all rabbits know how to dance. Humans have observed this ability and watched the mechanics of this dance for a long while. We know all too well how they speed up, throw their bodies into the air, and twist with the grace of an acrobat. The binky, as it is known among rabbit aficionados, has long been believed to be associated with happiness.

However, if you ask the rabbit, it's a gift and a prayer to the Moon Rabbit. Yes, the rabbit who binkies is a happy rabbit. But, just because they are happy, it doesn't mean it cannot be associated with something more. The wild abandon and joy of the movement is what makes it an act of reverence in honour of the perpetually leaping Rabbit of the Moon.

Stories of the Moon Rabbit vary far and wide. Everywhere there are rabbits, there is a different tale they tell. There's no barrier between wild rabbits and their domesticated counterparts, at least when it comes to this. The tales may well be told in a slightly different manner; that of the well-kept pet, especially those who stay indoors, is certainly more optimistic than that of a wild rabbit that lives in constant fear of being eaten. But, they still share the same hallmarks and characteristics. There are just too many to keep track of. If you took the time to ask one hundred rabbits, you would be almost guaranteed to get one hundred different stories in return.

How the Moon Rabbit lost its bark, but retained its bite. How the Rabbit of the Moon escaped the Fox of the Underworld. How the Rabbit found its way into the Moon. Why humans fail to comprehend the Moon Rabbit. How the Moon Rabbit kept his doe and kittens safe. How and why the Moon Rabbit placed the stars in the sky. Why the Moon Rabbit turns red as blood. How the Moon Rabbit taught his children to dance. Why the Moon Rabbit's twitching nose alters the weather. How the Moon Rabbit changes the season.

Each rabbit has his or her favourite story. Each rabbit is always eager for a willing audience. They would love to share it with you, if only you had the time to listen. After all, the hope that is imparted in each and every one of their stories is what keeps them hopping each day. It's what makes them search out the best grass, take risks, and throw themselves into the air. If an animal at such constant risk as a rabbit can find some joy in life, then there's no reason why anything else cannot.

I'm afraid that is all I can share for now. Some secrets, I have been sworn to take to the grave. I couldn't even bring myself to dare to break such a sacred vow. You have no idea what would unfold if I were to tell you certain things. Others? Maybe, on another occasion. First, I would need to ensure that it is safe to impart this knowledge to you.

How do I know all of this is true? I don't, not for certain.

But how do you know that it's not?

Butterfly Effect

Parvena twisted her black curls around her fingertips and fluttered her eyelashes in the boy's direction. He had a long, easy gait and loped towards her with the grace of a gazelle. She licked her lips and blushed crimson as she tore her gaze away. There was something about Justin Lawler that made Parvena go weak at the knees.

Justin placed his guitar on the ground and leaned against the fence beside her. He looked up at the sky, the rays lighting up his features. Parvena knew he was a sun-worshipper, and that he was grateful for any dry and bright day they had. It wasn't a surprise; the rain seemed like an almost constant feature here. Any day like this was a reprieve.

"Afternoon," Parvena said lightly. She drew out her necklace and started fumbling with it. "How was music?"

"Good," Justin answered with a grunt. "Broke a string, though."

"Ouch, I'm sorry."

"It don't matter. Got a spare at home."

Parvena nodded in agreement. Her stomach was in knots. She fingered the gem of her necklace more intently. It was a pretty thing; the stone was unusual. She never talked about it though, it was too precious to her. Parvena knew it was the most special thing she owned. She never went anywhere without it.

Still, she shouldn't have felt this nervous around Justin. Okay, so they hadn't known each other for too long, but she spent almost every waking moment with him. They enjoyed each other's company. They were friends.

In fact, she was almost convinced it was time. Time to tell him her greatest secret. She just hoped he wouldn't freak out.

"You're quiet today. You okay?" Justin asked softly.

He smiled at her and Parvena felt like her heart was about to give out on her. There was something about his lazy left eye and crooked smile that made her go weak at the knees. Parvena liked Justin for so many reasons, and she had long since lost track of what she thought was best about him. He was so sensitive and sweet. It may have taken him a little time to ask how she was, but he got there eventually.

"I'm fine."

Justin turned to face her. His floppy blond hair did nothing to obscure his scrutinising blue eyes. "You're a hopeless liar, Parvena. I don't know why you even bother trying."

"Shut up," Parvena answered stiffly. She clenched her necklace as tightly as possible. The edges of the gemstone dug into her palm. If she squeezed it any tighter, she would draw blood. "I'm bored here. Getting cabin fever."

Justin furrowed his brow and pushed his hair out of his eyes. "Well, it's not as if we can go anywhere. I mean, man, I wish I could. Hoping this baby will let me travel the world." He nudged his guitar gently with his foot. Parvena had heard him play; he was good, but that didn't necessarily mean anything. The creative arts were a constant battle. Even exceptional people could easily get pushed to the bottom without a second glance.

"Yeah, I have a far easier way of doing that."

"You don't happen to be a secret billionaire, hey?"

"Haha, I wish. Nah, it's..." she trailed off and toyed with the gem one last time. "It's this."

"That's your necklace. You always wear it. You love it almost as much as I love my guitar," Justin replied, obviously flabbergasted. "You're not on about pawning it in and flying around the world, are you?"

Parvena waved her right hand dismissively. Nobody would know how to value her gem. It was just a strangely coloured thing; it shimmered and altered as people watched it. It was attuned to her thoughts. It was almost like magic. "People just think it's a pretty trinket. You have to know the trick to get the best use out of it."

"What the heck are you on about Vena?"

Parvena shivered slightly. She felt like a cold spell had run down her spine. She loved it when Justin called her Vena.

"Anything you could wish for, it's just a hop, a skip, and a jump away."

"You're talking rubbish. Did you daydream through geography again or something?"

She shook her head violently. Her ponytail, already coming loose from a full day at school, whipped around wildly. Parvena felt sick. She should have known this was a bad idea.

But, damn it, she had been so very desperate to share her story with somebody. She trusted Justin completely. She hadn't trusted anyone besides her father in quite such a way before. She had believed that he would take her word for it. But he looked so unsure, so sceptical. How could she blame him? If somebody approached her and said the same things, then she would have thought they had lost it too.

"It's easy when you know how," Parvena urged. Justin sighed, bent down and picked up his guitar. "Please, don't look at me like that. I mean, honestly, I've done it tons of times before and it's really, really fun. There's just so much to see, so much to do."

"Vena, you're not making any sense."

"Why should we stay stuck here when we have the whole universe—multiple universes—at our fingertips?"

Slowly, Justin started backing away. His eyes darted in every direction. Parvena swore her heart was breaking. Justin's hand shook as he inched further and further away from her.

"Justin, please..."

"You really believe what you're saying, don't you, Parvena?"

"It's the truth." Parvena stared at the ground and her words came out as barely a whisper. Her hand clenched around the stone as it turned from a shimmering yellow to inky black. Tears pricked at the corners of her eyes.

"Well, I don't believe you. You're lying." Justin continued to stammer as he walked backwards. Even though he was freaking out, he never took his eyes off her. "I'm gonna tell everyone what a weirdo you are."

Her head hurt, or maybe she was just heartsick and the message was getting sent to her brain. Parvena wasn't sure if it made too much of a difference anyhow.

She opened her mouth and closed it again several times. Eventually, she said, "You wouldn't do that to me." Parvena's voice cracked as she spoke.

Justin dropped his guitar back to the floor and Parvena winced. The case may have been sturdy and strong, but she hoped that his precious instrument wasn't damaged. She watched, cautious, as Justin sat down beside his guitar and let his fingers run across the smooth leather case.

Slowly, tentatively, Parvena began to close the gap between them. She had to prove it to him, show that she was right. She wasn't a liar. This was a massive part of her life. It was something she had wanted to tell him about ever since they met. "No, it's true. Look, you only need a gem from another universe and then anywhere is a hop, a skip, and a jump away. I mean, anyplace, anywhen, anyhow."

"You're just being ridiculous."

"I'm not making this up. I thought you trusted me." Her plea was plaintive. Parvena wanted to reach out and touch him, but didn't dare. She wasn't sure whether or not physical contact would make a difference in this situation.

"I thought I did too. Then you started out with all this crazy-making stuff. I mean, really..." he trailed off, clearly losing his thought.

"No, it's true. Honest. Look, you know how the pages of a book are all squished together? Or how a filing cabinet is supposed to keep everything in order?" It was the best way she could explain it. It was the way her grandmother had told her about the gem and everything it entailed. "That's exactly what it's like."

"That sounds like something out of a science-fiction movie." He paused to pick at his cuticles before adding, "I'd watch it."

"I promise you, it's real."

"Yeah, sure, okay then." Justin's voice was laced with scepticism. He'd gone straight from denial and was now just humouring her. Vaguely, Parvena wondered if it would make any difference if she just disappeared in front of him right now. After all, there had been so many times she had felt invisible in this strange country, this strange world. She may have looked well-adjusted, and her new teachers may have been pleased with her progress, but it didn't change how she felt on the inside.

"Look, you know all those what-ifs, the ways things in your life could have been? That's exactly what it's like. There're billions and billions of different universes, each one following those 'what-if' moments. Like, what if the Titanic didn't sink?

What if my mom didn't die of cancer? What if some predator wiped out all of the human race's ancestors? Big and small, it's all out there."

Justin let out a hollow laugh. "No, this is definitely just some kind of weird story you've made up. It's all in your head." He grinned at her, happy with his explanation. Parvena wished he could know just how much it hurt to see him so disbelieving, so rude about what she was trying to say. He just didn't realise what he was doing. "You're always telling the best stories, Vena. You should go tell your English teacher. I bet you'd win a prize for it."

"I swear, it's not. This time, it's different." She was lying through her teeth now. Every other adventure—or misadventure—she had told him about, it had also been true. On those occasions, she had been happy to let Justin think it was a work of fiction. "I can't prove it to you unless you trust me."

"And how can I trust you when you are spouting out crap like this?" Justin shook his head. Parvena observed, silently. Her stomach was trying to gnaw itself from the inside out. Justin wasn't meant to react this way. "Vena, this just sounds like another one of your fantasy stories. Everyone wants to know what would have happened if their lives had turned out differently."

"It isn't made up." Parvena unfurled her fingers from around the gem. It fluctuated in colour between red, black, and blue, over and over. "You've always said there was something special about my necklace and there is." She paused, letting her words sink in. "This is what has all the answers. I don't know how it works, but it does."

Slowly, Justin reached out to touch it. Just before his fingertips made contact with it, he pulled away. Parvena could tell that he thought it was going to burn him or something. She spoke up again, "Haven't you ever thought of what could have been if something different happened in your life? Or if something else happened to the species as a whole? Haven't you ever wished you could jump to another place and see what could have been?"

For a second, Justin distinctly resembled a goldfish. Eventually, he sputtered, "Yeah, but who doesn't?"

"Well, this is your chance. I swear, I do it all the time and it's never done me any harm. In fact, I've made better choices here because of it."

"You really believe this, don't you?" His tone was low. She had finally worn him down. Parvena's heart skipped a beat and she grinned.

"Look, just humour me, okay?"

Justin shook his head again. "I must be going mad."

Together they entwined fingers. Justin grabbed hold of his guitar as Parvena pulled him forward. She took the lead; a hop, a skip, and a jump. There was a crackle of blue something around them, almost like electricity, but it didn't feel dangerous. For a brief moment, all they could see was blackness.

When they both opened their eyes, Parvena grinned toothily. All Justin could do was breathe, "Wow."

Yin and Yang

Our mother calls us, my sister and I, the Yin and Yang twins. It's not because one of us is mostly good and the other is mostly evil. At least, I don't think it is. Anyway, if that is the reason, then I like to think that I'm the mostly good one. Then again, my sister would say the exact same thing. I can guarantee that.

In the vast majority of ways, my sister and I are remarkably similar. That's not a surprise, considering we are identical twins. Almost everyone mixes us up. But, there are some very easy ways to tell us apart, at least physically.

I have a scar on my chin. I slipped over at the swimming pool when I was seven. Blood poured everywhere and Dad had to rush me to the hospital to get it stitched back up. My sister broke her right elbow a week later and there are scars all over it from where the bones poked out and it was pinned back together again. My right big toe, I nickname Frankentoe. A horse stood on it when I was twelve. My sister has shorter hair than I do. She likes to straighten hers. I can't be bothered to do that with mine. Instead, I prefer to cut myself in a fringe.

But yeah, I'll admit our personalities are similar. She prefers to read classic books, Bronte, Austen, that kind of thing. I prefer crime drama. She likes watching reality TV. I enjoy sport much more. She's more reserved than me and I'm clumsier than her. Still, people can't really tell who is who.

We enjoyed abusing it at school. Confusing the teachers and our classmates, pretending to be one another or clones or the same person with superhuman powers; it's all a part of the game. If you had a twin, I can guarantee that you would do the same, too.

But you don't need to go observing our reading habits, our music tastes, scrutinise our bodies for scars or anything like in order to tell us apart. All you need to do is look at the calendar, and figure out what time of year it is. Then, you'll probably be able to make a good guess as to who is who.

Iola, that's my sister, is currently outside. She's absorbing the sun's rays as if it is the thing that will keep her healthy year long. I honestly wish it would; I mean, who wouldn't? Isn't something we wish for on behalf of the people we love is to be healthy? I love my twin; Iola is my other half, she complements me, she completes me.

"Leora, come, come out. It's a beautiful day. We could have a picnic or go to the beach. Or, oh! Let's go to the zoo. Or something else, I'm cool with that. Come on, Leora. You don't want to be cooped up all day; it'll be fun." All summer, that's what she croons at my bedroom door. Sometimes she shortens it to Leo, but the use of my full given name is better for whining.

I cannot help but feel a little bitter over Iola's exuberance and joy during the summer months. It's something I cannot share with her. She may be an endless bubble of energy and enthusiasm, but I most certainly am not. The very idea of getting up seems like a wild and crazy way for me to spend the day. I'm sick, I'm tired and, mostly, I am bitter and angry at how I am wiling away the summer.

Don't get me wrong; lazy summer afternoons can be great, to some people. The idea of just lazing around and relaxing for hours on a time, it's like a joy. But that's not what it's like for me. People may accuse me of being lazy or antisocial or a bore, but it's not that I don't want to be doing things. I do, I really, really do. I just can't.

The sunlight alone is a problem. I squint and blink. It makes the backs of my eyes feel like agony. When you add the fact that noise is like a hammer going off right in my ear, it makes it worse. The fact my stomach feels like it's doing backflips—and not the good, butterflies of nervous excitement either—it's enough to make you feel sick.

Did I mention the pain? It's agonising, honestly. Imagine your worst headache, and then multiply it by ten. Imagine somebody has a vice around your head and they are squeezing it tighter and tighter. When you don't think it can get any tighter, it does. It feels like my head is going to explode.

This is how I feel every summer, without fail.

Thunderstorms, they only make it feel worse. Changes in the air pressure just make my whole head go haywire. The pain reverberates through my body and everything hurts. Just going to the toilet to throw up for the nth time is utterly exhausting.

It's a migraine. They are the bane of my life.

No, it isn't just a headache. Grinning and bearing it won't make a difference. I drink water like a fish. Paracetamol doesn't even begin to touch the pain. The pain isn't all in my head; it affects other parts of my body too. Working through it just makes me feel worse. Being optimistic is physically and emotionally draining.

Migraine is a genetic disorder. I inherited it off one—or both—of my parents. I wish I were just imagining it, then I could imagine it right away again. Everyone who has been blighted by this awful condition probably feels the same way.

You know what's insulting? People using it as an excuse to pull a sick day at work. Even if they do genuinely have them sometimes, it still makes me angry. It's such a devastating condition. It's literally ruining my life. Instead, people use it as if it were some kind of joke and nothing serious. I'd ask them to live a day of my life, but, well, I wouldn't wish this on my very worst enemy.

Not that I have any enemies, mind. I don't have the energy to go outside and make friends. And at times when I am feeling well, anybody I do meet ends up forgetting about me during the long periods I am absent.

Life's hard. I mean, I know there're people with far more difficult things to deal with than me, but with something like this, it's difficult to forget your own issues. It's not that I'm uncaring or self-absorbed; I'm just in pain and wish people would understand.

Even Iola forgets. That's why she tries to knock my bedroom door down every morning during July and August. She gets ill too, but she kind of forgets the pain. During the summer she glows and I fade away, like a ghost. We may have been identical at birth, in the womb, but there are still things we need to discover about one another.

If I could be bothered, I would write a diary. But the idea of writing seems too tiring. Besides, during the hazy months of summer, every day would have the same thing written: woke up, migraine, tried to sleep, vomited, bed. And so on, and so on, until the pressures of summer disappear in favour of a drizzly autumn and the long winter freeze.

I long for those days, the ones where I am not in constant pain. It's the thought of leaves falling from the trees, animals foraging before hibernation, grass covered by the first frost of the year and the first wintry snowflakes that mean I can get through the very worst of the summer heat. It just gives me hope that maybe, just maybe, I won't have to live like this for the rest of my life.

I mean, there's no cure for this. So many people suffer from it, but it doesn't mean that there's money to research it. I don't even have the most deadly migraine going—well, any migraine is deadly for self-esteem and mental health—but it's not like hemiplegic migraines. They look like strokes and they can kill. At least, that's what I've read. The idea of them alone scares me. At least my migraines aren't that bad, but there are people who aren't lucky enough to say that.

I just wish my sister could be a little more understanding, you know what I mean? Her footsteps sound like wild horses charging up and down the stairs. Her voice as she shouts, "Leo, Leo, Leora," through my wooden door is like nails through a chalkboard.

She's here again. Can't you hear her? "Leora, I do wish you'd come and be social. Leo, you must come and meet my boyfriend. I'm sure you'll love him."

A part of me is glad for her. She's out there, living her life. She's much better than she was last week. She had a migraine too; it only lasted a day, but believe me, a day is too long for anyone. However, the rest of me is jealous; I wish I were in her shoes.

Come autumn, though, I'll be okay. My migraines will dissipate. Maybe I'll even be able to go and get a holiday job or something over Christmas. Maybe I could meet somebody too. Who knows? I'll have to wait and see when the time comes.

You see, this is why our mother calls us the Yin and Yang twins. During the summer, I am mostly ill and Iola is mostly fine. During the winter, our roles are reversed.

We are identical twins and we both are tormented by this awful illness. We just seem to choose different times of year to be ill. It is the worst; I can assure you of that. But, there is nothing I can do. There's nothing anyone can do.

I only wish there was.

Between the Cracks

"I love you in that shade of pink."

Suzette could feel Blaine's eyes on her and spotted the dirty grin as it crept onto his lips. She scowled and grabbed her mascara wand. She didn't have time for this. After all, she was the vice president of the local charity for dementia awareness and she had a schedule that it was absolutely necessary she kept. If she didn't, then she would have appeared unprofessional in front of the rest of the committee. That was completely unacceptable.

Suzette jumped as Blaine wrapped his muscular arms around her waist. The mascara wand went haywire. When she opened her eyes again, Suzette could see that her face was ruined. Anger bubbled up in the pit of her stomach and she tried to swallow it down.

She did love her husband of twenty-three years, really she did. He was ruggedly handsome, gallant and an absolute rock for her. Suzette always knew he'd be there for her, no matter what went wrong. However, there were times when his behaviour was completely deplorable. He acted like an uncivilised caveman. This, of course, was one of those occasions.

Suzette whirled around in his arms. With her hand raised, she slapped him with full force across the face. His neck snapped back and just as quickly returned to its normal positioning. Grimacing, Blaine let go of her, and promptly started rubbing his sore cheek and staring back at her. He looked like a puppy that had been chastised for defecating in the house.

If she weren't so angry at him for bothering her, Suzette would have felt sorry for him.

"I'm busy, Blaine. Can you please get out of here," she grumbled. Suzette returned her attention to the mirror, picked up a makeup remover, and went about fixing the mess her darling husband had just made.

"But..." Blaine started. His reflection looked pitiful. Sometimes, Suzette couldn't help but wonder if she had married a man or a mouse.

"Out!" When she had asked him to leave, it wasn't a question.

Once Blaine slunk away miserably, it took Suzette twenty minutes to finish tidying up her appearance. Within an hour she arrived at the venue, only a matter of minutes before other members of the committee turned up.

On the way inside, she double checked how she looked in a handheld mirror. Somebody nudged her from behind and it slipped from her grasp. Suzette stared at the shattered pieces, aghast. She grumbled under her breath, but tried quickly to dismiss the superstition. Just because she'd broken her mirror, it didn't mean that she was about to get seven years of bad luck.

Within twenty-four hours, her husband was dead.

Blaine was allergic to bananas. It wasn't a common allergy; in fact, it was one he was often mocked for. But if even the smallest piece of banana slipped down his gullet, his throat swelled and he entered anaphylactic shock. He found it, frankly, embarrassing, and didn't divulge this secret to too many people. All he did was avoid bananas as best he could and keep his epipen on him in case of emergencies.

Suzette, of course, was perfectly aware of his affliction. When he'd informed her of it early in their relationship, she had found it vaguely amusing. Soon enough, she had learned just how serious it actually was—and not in an entirely pleasant way for Blaine. She had witnessed his allergic reactions on multiple occasions and now lived in fear of being widowed by a banana, of all things. He could see it in her eyes every time she read the word in a restaurant menu or walked past a fruit stall.

But, this evening, she had clearly put all thoughts of her husband aside. She was too busy with her committee, trying to raise money for a worthy cause, or something like that. Blaine wasn't entirely sure just how much of it he could take seriously. It was like she had taken charity in as her adoptive child.

Then again, he mused as he perused the cakes on offer at the late-night grocery store, it might not have been the case had they been able to conceive. Blaine had always thought if it happened, then it happened. Childlessness, meanwhile, had broken Suzette's heart. He considered himself lucky that he hadn't lost his wife in the process.

The cake he chose killed him.

It wasn't meant to include banana. Perhaps a lazy baker hadn't bothered cleaning his utensils to an adequate degree in between cake preparation and traces of banana were left in the chocolate chip muffin. As soon as Blaine swallowed, his throat reacted in the way it always did.

A first aider reached his side, but there was nothing she could do. Blaine didn't have his medication with him.

If only he hadn't left the epipen in his wife's care.

Suzette had believed that Blaine's funeral was going to be the most difficult phase of mourning. She was wrong. The funeral itself passed in a blur. The mourners were suitably upset and she felt a little less lonely that day. It was clear their friends and family missed him too. Half the community seemed to want to say goodbye.

No, the funeral wasn't as bad as she thought. It was the return to routine—the daily grind— *alone* that was the killer.

People talked about Blaine less and less. It was almost as if, now that he was dead and buried, they could erase all memory of him from their minds. Initially, Suzette's friends humoured her. They would reach out and pat her hand affectionately. They listened to her reminiscing, or at least pretended to.

Soon enough, the affectionate patting and willingness to talk about him dwindled. It was replaced with a heavy sigh or an eye roll. After that, people started to avoid seeing Suzette at all. She was just too depressing to be around.

She couldn't understand what was wrong. She had always made the effort to care for people. Suzette offered support to friends in hard times and delighted in their joy. She made time for the community as a whole. For some reason, she had always believed that care and attention would be reciprocated. Heck, if anything, other people owed her for caring.

Apparently, they didn't share her sentiment. The world as a whole judged Suzette for living in the past, for not being able to let go of Blaine. But they didn't understand; they couldn't understand her loneliness.

They couldn't understand her guilt.

After all, she had brushed him aside on that fateful night. She had acted as if his attention were worthless. She had been short and irritable with him. If only she had paid him a little more heed, then maybe her precious husband would still be with her.

Suzette had had his medication with her too. If she had remembered to pass it on to him before leaving, then maybe he would have had a shot at survival.

How could nobody else see that Blaine died because of her?

Over the years, Suzette disappeared into herself. As other people showed little to no interest in her despair, she saw no reason to spend her time with them. The house she had once shared with her deceased husband became her haven. Increasingly, she saw little cause to leave. She made excuses to stay home.

It didn't take long for people to stop calling at all.

It surprised her just how easy it was to turn from a social butterfly to a hermit. Once Suzette had dragged herself out of various social circles, people stopped associating her with them. Sure, she assumed that her name might come up in conversation every so often, maybe as an, 'I wonder whatever happened to that Suzette?' But that didn't mean those conversations went any further than that.

Certainly, it didn't turn into visits from those once-friends. It was almost like now that they didn't see Suzette on a regular basis, they could stop caring about her at all. As a consequence, her thoughts about these friends became bitter. They had taken her for a ride.

Suzette, meanwhile, wasn't lonely anymore. She didn't have a pet for company, not even a goldfish swimming around in a tank. She didn't talk to herself or hide herself on the internet, under a virtual persona. She didn't need any of that.

It was curious; the more she thought of her husband, the more she felt his presence.

There was a time when Suzette had scoffed at the idea of an afterlife. She'd believed people who talked about it were wishful thinkers and were fearful of their mortality. Death was the one thing guaranteed in life, and so many people spent all their time running from it. It was a waste of a life.

But, in solitary confinement, with time to think about her sins, it seemed like Blaine was trying to call for her.

The first hint was the full glass of water she put on her husband's bedside table. It was a routine of her old life, one from before she became a widow. However, three months after their abrupt separation by death, Suzette found the glass empty.

Every night since then, she had refilled it to discover it empty by morning.

It wasn't just water, though. She began to find Blaine's socks in the washing pile, when she hadn't even moved any of his clothes out of their closet. The computer betrayed her too; it showed e-mails being sent to her, from his private account. Each one she opened was empty, but somebody, something had to be pressing send at the other end.

It took just seven weeks for Suzette to grow used to these strange occurrences. She almost anticipated them. However, one night, she had been having a particularly vivid dream of Blaine when she woke up in the middle of the night. A cold sweat trickled its way down her back. She stared at the mirror she had placed opposite their bed. For half a second, she thought she saw the ghostly reflection of her dead husband disappear behind the frame.

"Blaine," she called. There was no answer. "Blaine, answer me. I know you're there." Her tone grew urgent.

Suzette closed her eyes and opened them again. The familiar figure of Blaine seemed to disappear out of sight as her vision focused. She inhaled. The scent of his cologne hung in the air. While she hadn't moved it off the dressing table, Suzette hadn't had any cause to spray any, not since that first year of grief. It felt sacrilegious, wrong. Why then could she smell it?

Her eyes stung and Suzette blinked furiously. Each time she opened her eyes, she swore she saw Blaine in the mirror. Craning her neck, Suzette looked behind her only to be greeted with a blank wall. She clenched and unclenched her fists several times.

If he were here, why then was Blaine just playing with her? Why wasn't he communicating with her properly? They had been apart for seven long years now, his death hung over her shoulders heavily, and yet he continued to taunt her. Every day, something reminded her of him. Seven years of oddities and reminders, it almost felt normal. But this, this was new.

She thought she saw the reflection of Blaine open his mouth.

In a pique of rage, Suzette hauled herself to her feet. She put both hands behind the mirror and in one swift movement sent it hurtling to the ground. Shards of the mirror sparkled back up at her, like glitter. Pearls of blood seeped to the surface of the skin on her foot, but Suzette felt no pain.

Her heart was beating fast and her pulse was racing. Suzette stared at the broken mirror, aghast. The last time she had broken a mirror was all too clear to her. She had been irritated by the loss of that old mirror at that committee meeting. Before now, she had never made the connection between the breaking of the mirror and her husband's death.

The shards twinkled up at her, all too temptingly.

It didn't help that each one seemed to show a different facet of Blaine's reflection.

Suzette picked up the largest one. It had the reflection of Blaine's mouth in it. She ran her finger over his lips, remembering how softly he kissed her. She recalled all the kind, loving words that fell out of them. What wouldn't she do to hear him say how much he loved her in that shade of pink all over again? What wouldn't she do to tell him that she loved him? What wouldn't she do to *be* with him right now?

It would be all too easy...

There was already blood on this mirror. What harm would it do to add a little bit more?

It wasn't as if there was anyone left to miss her, anyway.

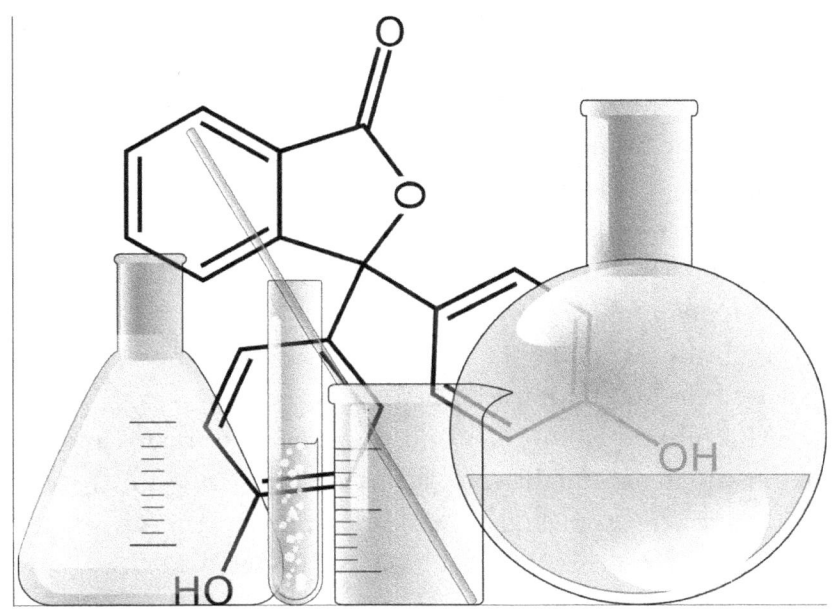

Hypothesise, Experiment, Repeat

in se est, quod melius erat volutpat.

What is the significance of that one-of-a-kind engraving which I commissioned and have displayed on my wall for many a year? Why, that is a rather simple question, do you not think? That is catchphrase for every single aspect of my life, from a molecular level right up to an entire being. In fact, I honestly believe that it should be the motto for every living being on the planet. That's not to say that those who are orbiting the planet should be excluded from this statement. Of course, as citizens and children of Earth, it is something that I wholeheartedly believe they should inherit too. It is their birthright as a member of the human race.

I'm sorry, I do have a tendency to digress. I have been led to believe that it is one of my few flaws in personality. But honestly, what do you mean you don't understand what *in se est, quod melius erat volutpat means*?

It really is quite a simple phrase to comprehend. It translates into 'strictly must do better next time.'

This phrase is succinct and appropriate for any and all situations that one might find themselves in. After all, is there any area where somebody cannot improve? The drive for perfection is a necessity for human survival. At least, my internet research informs me that this is the literal translation for this phrase.

I would elaborate on this hypothesis, and carry out deeper and more meaningful research into the translation. I could speak to classical students, converse with professors who happen to specialise in Latin, et cetera, et cetera. However, my time is something that is considered to be inordinately precious. One simply cannot afford to whittle it away on fanciful digressions such as languages to get to a position such as mine. There are far higher purposes to attain; I cannot waste too much time on pithy entertainment such as this.

I'm sorry? You believe I am continuing to deviate from the required course of this discussion? My apologies, but I was led to believe you sought me out on a quest for knowledge, a thirst and an appetite to learn. Conversing with those inherently superior to oneself, especially those with additional brain capacity, or at least a more efficient connection of neurons, is surely the best way to gain more insight, hmm?

Oh you media students are all the same. You're all pushy little know-it-alls who always have to have it their way. You have never been taught how to compromise, never mind learning to ascertain when something of higher quality than you originally intended is on offer. Did Mummy and Daddy finance the entirety of your higher education? And did they give you the keys to a shiny new car as they tearfully waved you goodbye? I trust you do not have to worry about crippling loans for the rest of your life, either, unlike the vast majority of your peers. After all, your pristine bag and shiny laptop say more about what is rattling between your ears than the words that have dribbled out of your mouth during this meeting thus far.

You see, some of us have had to work inordinately hard to get to the position we are now. We don't have the luxury of paying for a place in an educational facility such as this one. As a consequence, we have literally had to invest our blood, sweat, and tears in order to progress in life. Money talks, sure, but you certainly cannot pay for sheer talent. I guess that is why I am a professor of medical photonics and you are a mere slave of the media.

Sure, fine, walk away in a foul mood. I don't care if you go and have a cry about the sheer injustice in the world to Daddy Dearest. In the goodness of my heart, I agreed to this farce of an interview in the hope of spreading knowledge to the greater population. All you have done is waste my precious time; I simply cannot sacrifice any more of my energy on the likes of you. I have important work to do; my research will actually save lives. How honest, how pure is that, in the greater scheme of things? Meanwhile, you can carry on spreading gossip and hearsay as if it is the most important thing in the world. Media students, you're all the same. All looking to dig up the dirt rather than digging up the higher meanings of life.

So, we meet again. I am led to believe that I am expected to apologise for behaving in such a short manner with you on our previous session, but I do believe I made a valid argument. It is something that I hope you have dwelt upon and considered thoroughly. Has at least a portion of what I have said has settled within that pretty little brain of yours? Little being the operative word, of course.

Still *in se est, quod melius erat volutpat*, I say. Oh jolly good; you have managed to commit the translation to memory.

You... you mean to say you have a correction for it? You must excuse me, but I do believe you must be wrong. Still, at least you have done some research for this reprisal. As a consequence, you are already off to a better start than you were on our previous incursion. I wholeheartedly approve of this recent development. It is just a shame that you have chosen to dedicate your mind to such a fickle subject.

No my dear, I am not patronising you. Why would I ever do such a thing? What benefit would patronisation of you garner for one such as myself? Besides, I have been given strict guidelines to be cordial with you and answer all of your questions in a thorough and exhaustive manner. Honestly, I do believe that much of what I have to impart upon you will appear to be utterly incomprehensible to a mere media student.

Regardless, I have carried out a little research of my own and since been enlightened when it comes to the supposed importance of the student newspaper.

Although, why anyone would bother reading such trite fluff, when there are scientific journals for all interests available to expand one's capacity for thought, simply baffles me. Still, one cannot judge others for their tastes in fantasy and fiction.

Oh no, you misinterpret me entirely and that will never do. I do not mean to belittle the importance of fiction. A little otherworldliness, a brief daydream, is important for human beings. Without our flights of fancy, we would never be able to further our brilliant race. Besides, all the most worthwhile stories are simply life lessons in disguise, do you not believe?

However, many stories are just a reimagining of those that have already been told by superior wordsmiths. Others teach false lessons, ones which should not be encouraged in the youth of today. Many tales are honestly quite pointless. They are a waste of the paper they are printed on. Newspapers are designed with the lowest common denominator in mind; there is a reason that they say today's news is tomorrow's fish-and-chips paper. Not that I sully my body with such junk food as fish and chips. Like my brain, I like to treat my body with the respect it wholeheartedly deserves.

Now, now, there's no need to get so shirty with me. I am only establishing the base facts of our species. We need to live, we need to learn, and we need to do better next time. There is no point whatsoever in wasting time on idle chitchat and meaningless gossip. We live one life and it is our right—no, *responsibility*—that we use it to do the very best we can for the species as a whole.

The planet is in grave danger of being obliterated by mindless drones of people. Without due application of human abilities in key places, the planet on which we have been born into will be utterly doomed. As a consequence, even my research will be rendered meaningless in the greater scheme of things. The fact that I have advanced research in medical photonics and that my discoveries have, indeed, already saved many lives, will be rendered null and void. It is lamentable, but frankly, unavoidable unless the populace decides to change.

And yet, whilst I dedicate my life to saving people, you, the younger of the two of us with so much more to give, has opted to spread pithy stories about other people? There are so many meaningful vocations out there but you honestly believe your opinion is valid? I find that very thought ludicrous.

You're walking out on me again? My dear, you need to find a backbone. You won't get a shiny brass plate on an office door—like mine—with an attitude like that. It doesn't matter what you choose to study; without confidence in your vocation, you'll never get anywhere in life.

We meet again. Third time's a charm?' How cliché. Still if that is what you want to go with, I suppose it will have to do. I have already wasted far too much time bending to you and your whims. Let's get this interview done quickly, though I doubt you'll understand a word about medical photonics. It isn't something a media student can grasp in the space of half an hour, after all.

But still, I suppose you have shown some modicum of intelligence in each of the times we have crossed paths. You have also revealed that you have a steely edge, something which is required for a career in journalism, I suppose. I am led to believe you have some questions for me? Ask away, then. I haven't got all day.

Gardener's Envy

George Hutchinson peered over his five-foot-tall brown wooden fencing and let out a heavy sigh. His fingers twisted around trailing ivy leaves. They had taken years to train, but the effort had been worthwhile. The ivy, however, wasn't what was causing him discordance. George was well acquainted with the phrase *the grass is always greener on the other side*. Over time, he had grown accustomed to being that 'other side' which people eyed enviously. Instead, on this occasion, he was the one with a severe case of the green-eyed monster.

He didn't like this. Not one bit. It settled uneasily in his stomach, like a cabbage which had been attacked by slugs, leaving only tough stalks for human consumption. It made George feel bloated and more than a little bit sick.

Besides, it was incomprehensible for him to be suffering from gardener's woes. In fact, it was completely and utterly wrong. After all, he was George Hutchinson, gardener extraordinaire. There wasn't anything he didn't know about raising robust roses, beautiful begonias, tasty

tomatoes and dealing with devious dandelions. He was a prize winner; he had bountiful crops year after year. Neighbours always approached him for advice. And if they weren't after advice, they left with arms laden with nature's bounty—for a small fee, of course.

But this year, it was just going wrong and George couldn't understand why. The winter had been disastrously wet, turning has vegetable patch into a veritable swamp. His ornamental pond had overflowed, owing to the loss of life of three of his glass koi carp. Even his hardy annuals, which George had expected to bloom beautifully in the spring, had ended up being somewhat lacklustre compared to previous outings. His scattering of daffodils seemed to have been completely and utterly bamboozled by the strange weather patterns.

Weather wise, spring had been okay—a fair season. George had managed to get all of his planting done in good time and had already enjoyed a reasonable crop of radishes. But, thus far, that was the only crop he was having any success whatsoever with. Even so, it had been enough to give him a little optimism for the rest of the year.

Now, in early summer, things seemed to have taken a turn for the worse. Already, it appeared to be a scorching hot season. A poor amount of blossom on the cherry tree meant he would be starved of his favourite fruit come August. His water butt, which had been magnificently filled to the point of overflowing, was now looking a sorrier sight each and every day. The compost he was lovingly preparing for next season was being dried out. The radishes, which George had been led to believe that he could at least rely on, even they were beginning to shrivel up miserably. However much he trudged his watering can back and forth up his garden, it didn't seem to make a difference.

Across to the left, old Mrs Whittaker's garden looked worse than his own. That was hardly a surprise. Her husband, once a keen gardener, had long since passed. They had no kids to take it on and although the woman had tried to take care of it as her husband had, arthritis had scuppered her plans. Occasionally, George had offered his services to her, but she had politely declined. She claimed that she simply couldn't take advantage of him like that. It had been months since he had last seen the dear old lady. But, that wasn't troubling him either.

It was the sight over the other fence, the one to the right-hand side, which he had issues with. Whilst his lawn had taken on a crispy golden colour, hers was a lush green. George watched her on a daily basis, humming to herself while her dream catcher earrings brushed against her neck.

George paused to pull at his collar. Hippy chicks. What was it about them?

It wasn't just her who lived there, but two children, both brown from the excessive summer sun. She had a girl and a boy, who were constantly arguing or wreaking havoc with the rest of the kids from the neighbourhood. They were exactly the type who would wreck an award-winning garden without a second thought. That, again, was presumably the mother's fault. Those hippies just didn't understand the sheer importance of discipline in their offspring.

There was a reason why rose bushes required pruning, pea plants needed guidance up a frame, fuchsias feeding, and tomato plants stringing up to a firm stick of bamboo. It was all about order, making sure things grew up to be in the right place and look respectable at all times. Everything needed to be told what to do. Children, naturally, were no different.

In truth, the kids didn't bother George quite as much as the mother did. He didn't understand how and why this hippy mother with her flowing skirts, wind chimes, and dream catchers was having far more success with her garden.

He eyed her vegetable patch jealously as he watched her pick fresh spinach, rocket, chard, lettuce, and even a couple of plump tomatoes. George found himself having to swallow deeply, close his eyes and count to ten as the woman plucked an early strawberry, rolled it around her tongue and chewed. The sheer pleasure was evident on her face.

George found it strangely alluring as well as appalling.

The hosepipe ban was hurting him badly. If it weren't for the government insisting that there was a water shortage and behaving so pre-emptively, his garden would be as good as his hippy neighbour's. And if it weren't as good, then it would certainly have looked significantly better than hers. He would definitely have been in the running for biggest marrow for the fourth year in a row instead of the puny things he was stuck with now. His watering cans filled to the brim just weren't transporting the water quickly enough for his plants to survive.

For nights now, he had tried to catch the woman and her children out. They must have been cheating the ban, using the hosepipe at night when nobody was awake to see. George had toyed with doing such a thing, but had ultimately decided against it. He believed in fair play. If nobody else was allowed to use their hosepipe then why should he?

He turned away from her frankly enviable garden and wished he knew what her hippy secret was. George hadn't caught hide nor hair of an illicit hosepipe during his monitoring of the situation. In fact, he was becoming increasingly convinced that they didn't even own one at all.

As he closed his eyes, he could still imagine the cascade of mahogany brown hair falling over her face, obscuring her round cheeks and plump lips as her fingers toiled away at the soil underneath her. George knew that he should really stop worrying about what she was doing and just focus on his problems at hand. The green-eyed monster wasn't going to improve the state of his cauliflower and peppers any time soon, after all.

It was a week later and George was trying desperately to rescue a cucumber plant. Somewhat unexpectedly, he was startled by a husky female voice. He dropped his ball of twine and took a moment to compose himself.

His hippy neighbour had lived next door for three whole years and they hadn't once exchanged platitudes. He couldn't even think of a time when they had nodded hello at one another. The children, of course, were a different matter, but he had never found himself able to face the woman that had birthed the pair of them.

"Mr. Hutchinson?" she called again; her voice sounded a little tremulous this time. George turned around and stared at her. Of course, he had continued to monitor the Garden

Situation as he liked to call it, but he had never expected any change from the usual status quo.

As he stared into her hazel eyes, it occurred to him that it was also the first time he had ever had the opportunity to look at her face properly. A scattering of freckles decorated her nose and cheeks. There was a small mole just above her right eyebrow. Her nose was slightly crooked. Dimples had formed in her cheeks as she smiled, embarrassed, at him.

She looked tired. She also looked older than he expected. However, those damned dream catcher earrings added a cheerful, youthful whimsy to her whole appearance.

"I am ever so sorry to ask, but could I borrow your electric hedge cutters? Mine appear to have given up the ghost." She laughed delicately. It was the sound that George imagined angels and fairies would have made if they laughed and were, of course, real. "It's just my front hedge has gone insane what with all this sun and I really want to tidy it up before Mother comes visiting from Ireland."

She definitely wasn't lying about her problems with the hedge. Whenever George left the house, he looked disparagingly at it. He thought it lowered the tone of the whole neighbourhood, seeing it as wild as the children of the area were.

A strangled cry was the first noise to come out of George's throat. He pulled at his collar and swallowed again. He could feel crimson rising to his cheeks and was glad that he had a full beard to at least obscure his embarrassment, if only a little.

"Of, of course," he stuttered. She may have been the rival in his (mostly imagined) garden wars, but lending her his hedge trimmers was the gentlemanly thing to do. George had a reputation to uphold, even if his rival and sworn enemy was the one asking for a favour.

He hurried to the safety and security of his garden shed to pick up the requested tool. It was then that George realised exactly what he had to do. He simply had to know just how she had managed to keep her lawn so lush, her fruit crop so fruitful, and her vegetables such a verifiable success. He had to know where he, the experienced gardener for whom plants ran through his veins, had gone wrong. Most of all, George just wanted to know what the secret behind her success was.

George stood beside the fence, ready to hand the tool over, the hippy woman with her freckles, her brown curls, and her floaty skirt smiled warmly at him. Had he not been so preoccupied with his thoughts, he might have noticed it melt his heart just a little. Instead, he composed himself, ready to ask the big question.

"Just one thing before I hand these over." George cursed at himself; he sounded far too nervous. She was just a woman and he was merely helping her out.

"Oh?" she enquired and fluttered her excessively long eyelashes at him. George swore she would be the death of him. "I didn't realise that your Good Samaritan act came with strings attached."

George pulled at his collar. "I just want—*need*—to know how you are keeping your garden so healthy. This blasted drought is destroying years of hard work."

"Oh," she answered with yet another sweet laugh. "Is that all? It's simple, I recycle water."

"You...recycle water?"

"Oh, sure," she replied enthusiastically with a wave of her hand. "Dirty water from the washing up, water used by the kids in their bath; it's just that kind of thing. There's no point in wasting it all down the plughole when there are plants in desperate need of a drink, is there?"

George was dumbstruck. Her solution was so simple that it had been practically under his nose the whole time. Just how much water did he allow to drain away each and every day? She was right; it could easily be used for multiple purposes.

"Look, I'll get these back to you as soon as possible, but I really must get on." She waved the hedge cutters he had just handed over back in his face. It seemed like she was trying to take his eyes out with them. He would have taken a step back, but it felt like his mind wasn't in connection with his feet anymore.

"There's no need," George mumbled under his breath. "I can wait."

"All I can say is that I'll really owe you. I'll take you out to dinner to say thanks, yeah?"

"That would be very nice, but..." George started. He could feel himself going so red that even his beard wouldn't disguise it any longer.

"It's the very least I could do." She looked so earnest and reached out to touch his hand. George shivered in spite of the heat. It felt like an electric current had just run through his whole body.

Eventually, George couldn't keep his silence any longer. This situation was just wrong. He couldn't abuse her payment in kind, not like this. "I can't," he protested. "I don't even know your name." It was fact; ever since she and her children had rolled into the neighbourhood three years ago, they had always been known as Hippy Chick and her brats in his mind. He hadn't even taken the chance to get to know her properly.

"Oh, that's simple. I'm Amelie." Her name was clearly as beautiful as those hazel eyes of hers, George thought. "And you are... George, right? Well, George. I insist."

"Well..." he started, but was quickly silenced. Amelie leaned over the fence and gave him a quick peck on the right cheek. This time, George knew he resembled one of her tomatoes, the ones he wished he'd grown.

She began walking away but paused, tossing her mane of brunette curls over her shoulder as she did so. Amelie grinned exuberantly. The sun glowed around her. She looked angelic—there was no other way to phrase it. "Let's call it a date."

Earth Shaker

Alfreida gazed upon the world which was once her home and shook her head in disgust. Her ebony hair whipped across her face, obscuring the flash of brilliant emerald eyes. Whilst her face expressed irritation and disgust, her eyes showed fear.

The human race was developing. They were getting cleverer, scarier, and more destructive than ever before. Humans tore up the land with greedy viciousness and brutal ruthlessness. Everything was changing to fit their whims. There was no foresight, no consideration for anything but themselves. The superiority complex that each human seemed to have was indicative of their human privilege.

It was not a good time to be an elf.

Elves, historically, had always been considered a species superior to those Homo sapiens. Alfreida prided herself on her appearance; small pointed ears, sparkling eyes, and skin that seemed to glow. Her features meant that humans often mistook her for one of their kind, but elfkin could immediately tell the difference.

But, as Alfreida knew all too well, beauty was only skin deep. More important was her mind. She had knowledge and power that humans lusted over. She knew matters that human beings would kill over. Indeed, it was the kind of intellect that humans *had* killed over. Elfkin were a comparatively peaceful species, whereas the history of humans was decorated with blood.

For the longest time, she had looked on at the Homo sapiens with a disdainful sort of interest. It was the same with all elfkin. As long as humans kept to themselves and didn't disturb the elfkin, they rarely crossed paths. Even then, they were only mildly amused by humanity's antics.

Occasionally, a human would come to odds with an elf. Usually, this was unwittingly and the human always came off worse. Rarely, humans noticed this difference between themselves and the elfkin. In return, they offered homage, gifts to the elves. These were always gratefully received and the human in question usually obtained fond treatment in return for this common courtesy.

Times were changing. Humans had grown increasingly sceptical about the existence of elfkin. The few who still believed thought elves were little people who hid in shoes, or at the end of the garden. They thought elves would offer up their time willingly, without expecting anything in return.

Alfreida knew it didn't work like that. Cause and effect; you couldn't get something for nothing.

However, her clan had done nothing wrong. They hadn't deserved to have their home ploughed down to make way for diggers and concrete. Many had died needlessly; they had been sacrificial lambs to the slaughter. Humanity didn't even know— or care about—what they had done.

The forest hadn't just been home to elfkin; thousands of species had shared the land. Bluebells, bats, spiders, snowdrops, great oak trees, rabbits, foxes, elms, and more, had happily intermingled. Instead of reusing land that they had already claimed, people had destroyed a veritable paradise.

Alfreida bared her pointed teeth in response. The veins in her face purpled as a flash of red replaced the green in her eyes. Retribution was required. There was nothing else that could be said or done now. Her home had been rendered a desolate wasteland. The perpetrators were still out there, somewhere. They had to pay.

The elder of her clan had survived. Alfreida wasn't surprised to see him, nor him, her. She had sensed that he was around; a strange itching sensation at the back of her mind whenever and wherever she walked. In some ways, it was irksome. It distracted her from her end goal. In others, it was a comfort to know that she wasn't horribly, horribly alone.

"Come, my child, sit." He patted the plush cushion next to him. Alfreida knew that it was a demand, not a request. As a consequence, she begrudgingly acquiesced.

She didn't know the name that had been given to the Elder at birth; he had always just been the Elder to her. He had been a constant presence in the clan, a soothing influence. But how could he be a leader without a clan to control?

Alfreida didn't know how many other members of the clan had survived. No doubt, much of the flora and fauna had perished in the destruction. However, elfkin had the mental faculty to survive such a situation. But, in these few lonesome days since the discovery that her village and clan had been effectively erased, she had felt the presence of none but the Elder.

"You are troubled." His voice was soothing. Alfreida stared into his milky eyes. They were sightless; they had been for years. However, there were rumours and speculation that the loss of vision in the present had succumbed to vision of the future. When it came to the Elder, it was hard to distinguish between truth and lies.

Her eyes flashed red, but only for a second. "Of course I am," she retorted and punched the ground beside her with a balled fist. "Those humans have destroyed our lands. I will shoot an arrow into the heart of all who are responsible for this travesty."

The Elder chuckled. "You are as passionate as ever, Alfreida. But child, do I really have to consider confiscating your bow and arrow until you have learned to see some perspective in this plight?"

"An elf without her bow and arrow is nothing more than a fairy. She should be ashamed to ever be caught without it." Her veins were still pulsating purple. She watched the progression through her arms as she fingered her bow.

But, she was aware that the Elder was shaking his head sadly. She shrunk back into herself. "You are young, Alfreida. Please, you must learn to control your emotions. Flashing your colours will do no good in a situation like this."

Alfreida snorted. "Next you will be telling me I must assimilate myself with the Homo sapiens to ensure my survival."

"It wouldn't hurt," he acknowledged with a slight incline of his head. "But I know you have other abilities which allow you to... shall we say, blend into your surroundings?"

"What is it you wish me to do, Elder?" she asked tersely. She knew it was harsh to use such a tone with the Elder, for he was considered to be the wisest member of her clan. However, all he had done during this brief meeting was reprimand her for her just anger and frustration at this uncontrollable situation. Their home had been destroyed, and yet, he seemed like he was entirely at peace with the world.

"Calm down," he instructed. Alfreida rolled her eyes and flicked dark hair off of her face. "Your emotions are disturbing the balance. There is no need to be such an Earth Shaker, Alfreida."

Earth Shaker. Alfreida paced outside of the Elder's wigwam. Her anger, yet again, was reaching its peak. How dare the Elder call her an Earth Shaker? All she wanted was payment in kind for what the humans had done to her home.

Long gone were the times when elfkin carried out interspecies relationships. Long gone were the half-elfkin, half-human offspring which had resulted from these brief unions. The elfkin were under attack from a fellow bipedal species, one which had the audacity to label itself as clever.

Elfkin were meant to adhere to nature's laws, to encourage balance in the ecosystem. Alfreida had had those lessons drilled into her since birth. However, sometimes there needed to be time for action. She couldn't just lie in wait for the danger to pass. Why else were elfkin trained rigorously in the art of archery, if not to actually use their weapons? After all, they were deadly. They weren't just ornamental reproductions to be admired from a distance.

Alfreida wasn't being an Earth Shaker; she wasn't looking to damage the worlds beneath her feet unnecessarily. She was looking to save them, before it was all too late.

If that caused some ripples in the here and now, then who was she to be judged? It was impossible to move through the planet without having some kind of an effect on it. Birth and death alone each had their own unique set of repercussions. If anything, that meant every single living thing was an Earth Shaker, right from conception.

She threw back her head and shoulders. Then, she straightened up her bow and counted her arrows. Alfreida could practically taste the blood in her mouth. It was time for retribution.

The sound of snapping twigs and crunching leaves filled her pointed ears. Alfreida backed her way towards a mighty willow tree. It was in its winter dress; the saddest time of the year. The feel of the bark underneath her fingertips quietened her heart. She focussed on her breathing and closed her eyes.

When she opened them again, just seconds later, she knew she was invisible to all but other elfkin. Her camouflage skills had long been considered the best of her generation. Alfreida prided herself on her ability to disappear against any surface.

Still, that was the past. For now, she had to focus on the present. That meant identifying whether or not the approaching footsteps were that of friend or foe.

The two individuals came into view. A boy and a girl; they couldn't have been much older than fifteen. Slowly, she selected an arrow out of her quiver and placed it against the bowstring. The moment they came into sight, she knew they weren't elfkin.

"Parvena, where exactly are we?" the boy grumbled.

Alfreida steadied her breath. Every movement, she kept deadly silent. Slowly, she pulled back the arrow until the string could take it no further.

"I don't know, but we're not home," the girl, Parvena, replied quietly.

Alfreida cocked her head to one side and let the muscles in her arm relax. These two children in front of her, they looked like humans, they smelt like humans, and they acted like humans. But, their auras seemed wrong. They looked like they were completely out of step with the world around them.

Closing her eyes, Alfreida wished for an answer. Nothing was coming to her; nothing except *wait* and *watch*. The Elder was right; she couldn't rashly kill these babes. Even if their parents were the ones responsible for destroying her home, killing her brethren and the simple species of the forest, she couldn't kill the young.

In addition to that, their auras were peculiar and unfamiliar. These children needed more investigating. How did they get here, where did they come from? They would be unable to answer questions if they were deceased. It didn't matter how much vindication Alfreida would feel over their deaths.

Besides, their sheer presence was unnerving. It felt like a greater war was about to emerge. The earth beneath her feet felt like it was shaking, and this time, it wasn't the doing of an elf.

Alfreida knew what she had to do now. The Elder was right; the moment she had been thrown off by these new visitors and calmed down, she had discovered a purpose which she wouldn't have noticed before. She had to track down as many elfkin as possible; even closely related species, the fairies, the gnomes, and the dwarves. Whatever it was they were about to fight, they had a decision to make. Together they would stand, or else they would fall. These bizarre new children were a sign of the troubles to come.

They might not have been portents of doom in themselves. Parvena and the boy might even need guidance to find their home. If they were innocent, no doubt the fairies would argue it was their responsibility to help. If they were dangerous, the gnomes would be furious that Alfreida didn't kill them when she had the chance. Whatever the case, there was an innate wrongness about them, their colours and their presence, and that in itself was a sign of danger. It also indicated that this was something she had no right to deal with alone.

With a flash of black hair, Alfreida disappeared. She couldn't delay anymore. It was time to fulfil her destiny. If it led to the world settling back into the natural order of things afterwards, it didn't matter if her actions led to the shaking of the earth on this occasion.

One for Luck

Arthritic fingers scrabbled amongst the coins in her purse. Every movement sent a spasm of pain from fingertips, through hands, then up her arms and shoulders. It only ended right in her very heart. But she persevered. She had to. It was something that she had to do each and every single day.

Until he came home. That's what Irene Whittaker promised herself, and promised him. She'd keep up this routine until her Tommy came back home.

She rubbed the dirty bronze penny against her sleeve, ignoring the pains that jolted her joints. Carefully, she lifted her hands up to her lips and pressed them against the coin. Squeezing her eyes shut, a tear escaped and trickled down her right cheek. A whole waterfall of tears had fallen in this spot by now. They would have drowned out the orange linoleum of the porch if they had all been shed at the same time.

Her hand hovered briefly over the transparent jar before the coin slipped through her fingers and landed with a loud jangle along with the many others.

Irene Whittaker had carried out this weary action every single day since her son had gone to war. He'd insisted it was his civic duty and he had to defend human rights. He said it was for the good of the nation and the only honourable thing he could possibly do.

She had let him go. He had given her no choice in the matter. Tommy was an adult and it was his decision to make.

Irene had told him to write often, to stay safe, to look after himself, and come home alive and well. That was all she had ever wanted for him.

After he left, she heard from him just the once. The letter he sent was safely folded into her purse. She never went anywhere without it.

Tommy hadn't even married by the time he slipped through her fingers. She had no grandchildren to hold onto whilst their father was away and fighting with the military. Fighting for good, if Tommy were to be believed. Irene had lived through too many wars to believe that any good could truly come from it.

The one thing Tommy had done was present her with a small glass jar. He had then taken out a coin and dropped it inside.

"One for luck," he'd murmured. Irene could still hear his words rattling in her brain, even now. Her hearing may have been on its way out, and her eyesight only in marginally better condition, but she could still see and hear her son. Irene's memories of him would be with her until her dying day.

The day after he left, she had dug out her own coin and followed his lead, just as she had promised.

Tommy hadn't come home, so she never stopped putting her coins in jars.

Missing in action didn't mean the same thing as *dead*. She had to cling onto the vain hope. It was all she had left.

That original glass jar had been filled long ago. Irene had replaced it with different jars time after time, filling each one. Her collection of jars and coins mapped the years. The changes in the currency, the different heads of state, imperial and decimal coins, they all sat in her porch, lining the shelves.

They marked the passage of time, the time Irene and her son had spent apart and a lifetime of hope. Irene's glass jars of pennies were almost as much a part of her as her heart was. She couldn't survive without either.

She retired back into the house as quickly as her aching knees could carry her. Rain plastered the windows and winds howled. It was a miserable autumnal day. Nobody in their right mind would go out in this weather.

But Irene had. She placed her newly-purchased loaf of bread on the kitchen counter before slipping her jacket, hat, and scarf off in the hallway. All were black, the colour of mourning. It was only appropriate for a decrepit widow such as herself.

Richard Whittaker, Irene's beloved husband and father of her only child, died around ten years ago. Irene had lost count of precisely how long it had been since he'd passed on. She was the only one left in her family, the only one left who could be bothered to care about the fate of young Thomas Whittaker.

Her heart ached for both her husband and her son. Cancer had stolen Richard away, though Irene secretly believed that he'd just grown bored with her. Bored and irritated with her vain hopes that her son would come wandering back through the front door, as if he'd merely been off for a ramble through the fields. They had never been able to see eye to eye about Tommy's fate. Other things, they could compromise on, but Tommy was simply not one of them.

She sighed heavily. Irene was cold to the bone. Her body was wrecked with pain. Her heart, filled with loneliness and sadness. These were the norm. This was all she'd known for too many days, weeks, months, even years.

Briefly, her watery brown eyes lingered on the door. There would be no visitors today. There never were.

Once the household chores were done, Irene sank into her old, overstuffed armchair in the lounge. Days like this, it felt like living was just too hard. She closed her eyes and allowed herself to drift off into a dreamless sleep. It felt like dreaming her life away was the only thing she was good at now. Any skills she had once had, any work she could once do, it had all been laid to waste. Society deemed that Irene Whittaker and her irrepressible hope for her son were now utterly worthless.

"Mum?"

Irene's eyes flew open. She felt like she had only just closed them. But, there he stood, her beautiful baby boy.

His black felt cap almost covered up his beautiful blue eyes. Those, he had inherited from his father. His skin was smooth and clear, just as it had been on the day she had tearfully waved goodbye to him. Tommy wore that all-too familiar lopsided grin; pleased to be home. The deep green uniform looked too big for his body, but the polished brass detail proved that he wore it with pride.

Irene's heart warmed. Her son had finally come back for her. Nobody had believed her; they had decided that it was just the ravings of a sad, lonely old lady. Some people humoured her for a brief while, but eventually everyone just gave up on her.

But Tommy, holding out his hand for his mother, had proved them all wrong. Irene accepted his hand. The moment she was on her feet, she wrapped her arms tightly around his slender waist. She inhaled his scent, felt the warmth of his solid body underneath her fingertips. Tommy fit inside her arms as he always did. Finally, after so long, Irene felt like she was complete again.

Something clattered in the back garden. Irene didn't notice; quite frankly, she didn't care.

Jonah looked warily from left to right, scared that he would get caught prowling in old Mrs Whittaker's back garden. But he wanted his football back and his brother was way too chicken to come get it. Besides, it was raining and their mum had told them not to go play outside.

His eyes lingered on Mrs Whittaker's porch full of old coins and the back door. It was open. Mrs Whittaker never left her back door open.

Curious, the young boy dropped his ball and edged towards the porch. The orange linoleum was muddied and the coin collection freaked him out. His hands shook. Swallowing down his fear, he stepped through the porch and inside the back door.

"Mrs Whittaker?" he called. "Mrs Whittaker, it's Jonah Carter, from next door. Mrs Whittaker, are you here? Your door was left open and..." he trailed off as he wandered into the old lady's lounge.

The television blared, but nobody was paying any attention to it. Mrs Whittaker's handbag was sitting beside her old, fraying armchair. Her purse had fallen out, spilling its contents across the floor. A piece of paper, decaying with age, was just by her foot.

"Mrs Whittaker?" he asked once more.

She didn't move. She didn't know he was here. Her eyes were closed and there was a pleasant smile on her old and usually dour face. Jonah took a couple of steps back and swallowed deeply. Then, he turned on his heels and ran. He was just a kid; there was nothing more he could do. But he had to tell someone, even if he didn't want to.

Jonah ran straight home and reluctantly confessed all to his mother. He cringed as he spoke, believing that at any moment he would be chastised for not following her instructions, for trailing mud through the house and for trespassing next door. But, instead, she twisted brown curls around her fingertips and listened sagely to what he had to say. His heart thumped wildly in his chest until she patted him on the head gently. She smiled, stroking his hair before whispering, "It's okay, Jonah. She is at peace now."

This story is dedicated to the twenty individuals who backed my Kickstarter campaign. These people made the publication of this collection of short stories become a reality.

Cold Like Ice

"Hey, Nora, what's a pretty girl like you doing at a crime scene like this?"

Nora Lynne Wittry flicked a few loose strands of hair out of her eyes and grimaced. Barely a day went by without a catcall or a look of disbelief. Still, she ran her fingers over the badge that rested on her hip. She had every right to be here. In fact, her assistance had been requested. Ergo, the sexist bastards could shove their stupid comments up their asses. She was good at her job and that was what counted.

Using the red brick wall as purchase, she slipped and slid her way to the local sheriff. Nora Lynne may well have loved her job, her home town, and the people in it, but that didn't mean there weren't downsides. For one, the most obvious

thing glaring her in the face: murder. It may have kept cops like her in a job, but it didn't mean it was something she necessarily wanted to see. Then there was the weather. Living in a northern state, where the snowy weather started too damn early and receded far too late, was a pain the ass, especially when it came to getting around.

Still, it was something she had learned to live with all too long ago. However, that didn't make it any less annoying.

She smiled wryly when she finally found herself opposite the sheriff and proffered her gloved hand. "Sheriff Novak, it's good to see you again." As she talked, her breath was visible. Quickly, Nora glanced upwards. It looked like another dusting of snow was on the horizon. She couldn't decide whether or not that was a good or bad thing. The sidewalk, after all, had become an icy death-trap and the nearest ER had been awash with broken bones and the elderly and infirm coming in with pneumonia and a bad case of the flu.

It was just a shame that the weather couldn't quell the crime rate at the same time.

"Nora, I mean it. Shouldn't you be at home knitting or cooking up a pot roast or something like that? Are you sure that your delicate eyes can handle a bloody murder scene like this one?"

"Sheriff Novak, please remind me why you continue to employ an idiot with mud for brains like Hopkins here?"

Sheriff Eric Novak bit his lip and wrinkled his nose. Nora could tell that he was desperately trying to stop himself from laughing. Unlike many men in his position, Eric wholly disapproved of sexism in the workplace. He liked and respected

Nora. It may have had something to do with being his niece, but Nora knew he treated all women within the force as his equals.

"Unfortunately, Detective, my superiors saw it fit to foist the idiot Hopkins on me." Finally, he let out a toothy grin. Nora frowned when she noticed one of his middle teeth was missing. "But, I do have to concede that his brawn can come in useful sometimes."

"Sometimes," she echoed; scepticism dripped off of every syllable.

"Yeah, like splitting up brawlers in a bar fight. Taking down motorcycle gang members, crap like that."

"So you're saying he has had all of his brain cells knocked out of him, then?"

"Yeah, sure, something like that."

Hopkins' face fell. "Hey, that's way harsh."

"Can it, Hopkins," Nora retorted. "If you can dish it out, you can take it too."

"Harsh, but fair," Eric conceded. "But we have a crime scene to attend to."

The red brick house was a bit of a disappointment once inside. No central heating, detritus lying in every direction, and a heavy smell in the air. In short, it was the perfect place to dump a body. A damned shame, really, Nora considered. From the outside, it looked like this house could make a lovely family home.

"Hey, Nora, your head looks like it's on fire," Hopkins started and in unison, both Nora and Eric rolled their eyes. It was a terrible family habit; her mom always told her if she kept it up, her eyes would fall right out of her head. "Can't you do something about the temperature of this building?"

Nora, a natural redhead, with a dusting of freckles across her nose, and haunting green eyes, had heard it all before. She couldn't say the words didn't hurt, but over time, she had learned to brush it off faster. On the plus side, the abuse she had received as a child courtesy of schoolyard bullies had toughened her up nicely.

Naturally, Nora considered everything she had achieved thus far to be payback. In the earlier days, when she walked the beat, she took great relish in slapping speeding fines and wrapping handcuffs around the wrists of those who taunted her as a kid. Some people never grew up and, although she never told anyone, it felt like just desserts to punish them after all this time.

Still, Hopkins' comments were neither unexpected nor wanted. They were beginning to get under her skin. "How many times do I have to tell you to shut it?" she growled. Eric appeared not to hear; he was trudging up the rickety staircase already, with one hand gripped firmly around the bannister.

"I will if you go on a date with me," he answered and pressed a hand in the small of her back. Nora moved away from him quickly.

"Maybe when hell freezes over," she muttered. The fact that she was engaged—and had been for the past four years—notwithstanding, Nora knew she'd never date a brainless oaf like Hopkins. She had more self-worth than that.

When she reached the top step, Eric was waiting for her. He looked sombre; justifiably so considering this was a murder case. Beyond that, she had little knowledge of what to expect. Her fingers tingled; an adrenalin rush.

"Forensics have been and gone," he warned her. "Nora, there's something I should tell you..."

Nora cast her uncle a furtive look, but stepped beside him and pushed the door open.

The door creaked as it swung slowly open, revealing the body. Stuck in the middle of the trash, like he'd been cast out on a dump, it had already started to head into a state of decay. However, the features of the face were still recognisable.

"No," she breathed. "No, it can't be. He's still missing, he's..." she trailed off as Eric placed a hand on her right shoulder.

"I'm sorry, Nora. It *is* your father."

The silence was deafening as his words echoed around in her brain. With that, Nora's whole world was crumbling down around her.

Acknowledgments

Writing is meant to be a solitary experience, but nobody can get very far with it alone. As a consequence, I would like to thank the following people for assisting in the creation of *Odds & Socks*.

Emma Brown, Lionel Cowell, Conny Hempel, Mega Cowell, Peter, Janet and Richard Doland, Kim Britton, Stephanie Hood Wittry and Rachel Cheng for their generosity and endless support. Nick Wahlstrand, Amy Harris, Fiona Bond, Elisa Balestri and Andrea Miller, all of whom have helped me in one way or another over the years. My creative team: T. Morgan Editing Services for smoothing the rough edges and making me look better than I am. April Sanders, my graphics artist. Also, Mark McKnight for taking a chance on me.

Thanks to my family for letting me take the time to find myself as a person and a writer. For giving me the space to fight my health. For letting me be the writer I want to be.

Finally, to you, the reader, for picking up this little book, giving it a chance, and getting to the end.